Walt Disney's
Toad Flies High

With characters from the Walt Disney motion picture
The Adventures of Ichabod and Mr. Toad.
Adapted from *The Wind in the Willows* by Kenneth Grahame.

A GOLDEN BOOK, New York
Western Publishing Company, Inc.
Racine, Wisconsin 53404

One golden summer day Mole, Ratty, and MacBadger set out across the river in Ratty's boat. They had a picnic basket, and they were thinking happy, hungry thoughts.

"It's a lovely day for a picnic," said Mole. "But wouldn't it be more fun if Toad were here?"

Vroom! A red streak flashed by.
It was a motorboat, and Toad was at the wheel.
The waves rocked Ratty's boat until it almost sank.
"Toad, look out for the—"
Mole started to shout.

Too late, Toad saw a log floating just ahead. There was a
terrible crash, and the beautiful red motorboat sank like a stone.
Toad sat in the shallows and trembled with excitement.
"Oh, my! Oh, joy! Oh, Toad, what a splendid fellow you are!"

"Splendid?" snapped Ratty. "You're not splendid."

"You're a disgrace!" scolded MacBadger. "You've gotten us all wet, and you've ruined our lunch!"

"I am truly sorry," Toad said, for he really had meant no harm. "Please forgive me. But that wonderful boat . . ." A dreamy expression spread over his face. Smiling, he climbed out of the river and went off to Toad Hall to change his clothes.

Mole sighed as he watched Toad go. "I wish I'd had just one ride in the motorboat before it sank," he said to himself.

The next day Mole, Ratty, and MacBadger set out again, with a second picnic basket. This time they hiked across the meadow to the high road.

"We should have invited Toad along," Mole said.

Suddenly there was a loud roar. Around a bend sped a shiny red motorcar, with Toad in the driver's seat.

"Watch out!" shouted Ratty and MacBadger.

Mole leaped aside, dropping the picnic basket, as Toad zoomed past. With an ear-shattering crash, the shiny car rammed right into a tree.

There amidst the wreckage sat Toad, still gripping the steering wheel and jiggling up and down as if he were driving.

Ratty got a hatful of water from a nearby stream and poured it over Toad. Toad shook his head and blinked his eyes. He looked around at his three friends.

"Shocking!" cried MacBadger. "You've smashed the car and you've smashed the tree!"

"You've smashed our lunch, too," said Ratty.

"I *have* been wicked," admitted Toad. "Very well. No more motorcars for me! No more crashing into trees, either." To prove his good intentions, he got right to work cleaning up the mess.

"Perhaps he has learned his lesson," said Ratty.

"Let's hope so," said MacBadger.

Mole said nothing, but he sighed. The motorcar had been very beautiful, and Mole had never ridden in a motorcar. "Perhaps I never shall," he thought sadly.

The next day Mole, Ratty, and MacBadger set out once again, with a *third* picnic basket.

"Did you invite Toad?" asked MacBadger as they started down the lane.

"I tried to," said Mole, "but he wasn't home."

No sooner had Mole said this than a
thundering noise from overhead startled
the three friends.

"Good heavens!" cried Ratty.

"It's Toad!" said MacBadger.

"In an airplane!" shouted Mole. Again
he dropped the picnic basket.

"Glorious!" Toad sang out as he looped the loop in his magnificent red airplane. He waved cheerfully to his friends below.

Crash! The airplane came to a sudden stop in a haystack.

"Toad, all this racing about must stop!" shouted MacBadger.
"For shame!" said Ratty. "What a sight you are, sitting there blowing hay out of your nose!"

Toad hung his head. "Don't be angry, please, Ratty," he begged. "I promise to stop flying airplanes. In fact, I'll stay away from motors altogether—for a year and a day, at least."

Toad picked up the broken bits of his airplane. Then he tidied the haystack.

Mole felt sad as he watched Toad. The airplane had been truly marvelous, and he'd never had a ride in an airplane. "I suppose I never shall," he thought glumly.

The next day Ratty, MacBadger, and Mole tramped across the fields to the far meadow. Mole took the picnic cloth from the *fourth* picnic basket and spread it on the grass. Ratty set out the sandwiches. MacBadger sliced the cake.

Suddenly Ratty shouted, "Run for your life!"

A large, angry bull was galloping straight toward them. They ran for a tree.

Suddenly, just when all seemed hopeless, there was Toad! He was dangling from a rope ladder attached to a gigantic hot-air balloon! Toad waved a large red handkerchief at the bull.

The bull turned and charged at the handkerchief. Toad floated upward, safe from harm, as his friends scrambled up the tree and out of danger.

The balloon drifted toward the tree. "No motor, you see," said Toad as he helped his friends up the ladder.

"The balloon is every bit as nice as an airplane, Toad," said Mole. "How kind of you to rescue us and give us a ride!"

"It was nothing," said Toad. "However, I do have another surprise for all of you."

He uncovered an elegant picnic basket, stacked high with good things to eat.

"Why, Toad," said Ratty, "we shall have our picnic after all! You *are* a thoughtful fellow!"

After a pleasant lunch, the four friends floated happily home.

In the days that followed, Ratty, MacBadger, and especially Mole enjoyed many glorious rides in Toad's wonderful balloon.

And what of Toad's promise to stay away from motors? Well, he did keep it—for exactly a year and a day. After that? Well, you know Toad....